BLACKBEARD

BY PAT CROCE

Illustrated by Tristan Elwell

RP CLASSICS

PHILADELPHIA · LONDON

Library of Congress Control Number: 2010940371

ISBN 978-0-7624-3673-6

Designed by: Ryan Hayes
Typography: Baskerville Book and Phaeton

Published by Running Press Classics
an imprint of Running Press Book Publishers
2300 Chestnut Street
Philadelphia, PA 19103-4371

Visit us on the web!
www.runningpress.com

STANDING on the stern of his ship with a spyglass extending from his right eye, Blackbeard clearly distinguished the flags of the Royal Navy's HMS *Scarborough* fluttering in the distance. He watched anxiously as the sailors aboard the 30-gun man-of-war were making ready for battle.

"Israel," Blackbeard said, with his eye still fixed on the dreaded naval vessel, "it looks like we have a heap of trouble heading our way."

"What do you see, Captain?" Israel asked.

"I see a British Royal Navy warship off our port side and closing distance upon our quarter. There are marksmen scurrying up the rigging into the crosstrees with muskets strapped across their backs. The gunports are open and all of her cannons are run out and ready. And I spot officers on the quarterdeck distributing swords and pistols to those blasted striped-shirt sailors," said Blackbeard.

"Let's show her our heels and sail away as fast as we can!" Israel exclaimed. "We have the wind in our sails. And according to my calculations there are only a couple of hours of daylight remaining, so we can easily disappear into the night. And Blackbeard, you know that no pirate vessel has ever engaged in a fight with a naval frigate!"

"Well, Mr. Hands, it looks like you might make history," Blackbeard said, as a devilish smile creased his face.

Israel Hands was shaking his head as he stared solemnly at the horizon. He was Blackbeard's loyal first mate, a navigator by trade, and not particularly interested in doing battle with an English warship. The navy hanged pirates!

Blackbeard lowered the spyglass and shouted, "All hands on deck!"

The ship's quartermaster, Black Caesar, maneuvered his way through the hundreds of pirates moving on the main deck of the Caribbean's largest pirate ship, *Queen Anne's Revenge*. The sailing ship was a beautiful three-masted vessel that Blackbeard had fitted with forty guns. There was an array of large cannons lining the gun deck and smaller swivel guns mounted on the gunwales. She was one of the rare pirate ships that had the firepower to compete against the likes of the *Scarborough*.

"What's all the alarm about, Captain?" asked Black Caesar.

Black Caesar was an escaped slave who had earned Blackbeard and his crew's respect and was elected as the ship's quartermaster to represent their interests—such as distributing food, rum, and money, overseeing punishments when necessary, and deciding what plunder would be removed from captured prizes. The captain had no say in these matters. He had absolute authority only in time of battle, which looked increasingly closer by the minute.

"Caesar, we have an important decision to make," said Blackbeard. "On the horizon we have a Royal Navy vessel giving chase and slowly closing upon us. We must put to vote whether we flee or fight."

Blackbeard watched from the quarterdeck as the entire crew of three hundred tough, scarred, cutthroats assembled throughout the main deck to decide his fate.

"How did I get here?" he thought. "One day I'm fighting for the Crown and the next day I'm fighting the Crown's navy."

. . .

AS A YOUNG BOY growing up in the coast town of Bristol on the southwest side of England, Edward Teach played with salt air in his black hair and sea air in his red blood. He would hang around the old wooden docks and question the sailors and merchant seamen about their many adventures in faraway lands.

"Where did these bales of cotton come from?" asked young Edward, looking at the cargo being unloaded from a ship onto the dock. "And what are these large brown leaves? They stink!"

"We just sailed for weeks across the Atlantic Ocean from America," replied the sailor. "The cotton came from a place called South Carolina, and the stinky leaves are from the region due north in North Carolina. It is called tobacco."

The crew members enjoyed the energetic boy's curiosity and courage, so they taught him the ways of a sailor. He was quick to learn how to make sailor knots and read a compass. They showed him their navigation methods of sailing across the open seas. And since Edward was big and strong for his age, they even showed him how to handle a razor-sharp sword and how to load and aim a pistol.

"Why do you need pistols when you have these guns onboard?" asked Edward, patting one of the cannons.

"The big guns are good for scaring smaller pirate ships away," said the sailors. "But in case we are boarded by a large band of pirates, we must be able to defend ourselves."

"Let pirates attack when I am aboard," said Edward, slashing and stabbing the sword as he had been taught. "I will teach those rogues a lesson they will never forget."

In the year 1702, when Edward was about twenty years old, Queen Anne of England declared war against her neighbors France and Spain. And to help support her naval fleet, England authorized private ship owners with a commission known as a "Letter of Marque" to openly attack enemy ships. Mother England permitted the privateers to keep 80 percent of their plunder and forward the remaining 20 percent to her treasury.

It was a kind of legalized piracy.

Edward began his sea adventures based out of Port Royal, Jamaica. It was during this period of his life that he learned the tricks of the plundering trade. He was a natural-born leader and because he was tall, strong, smart, and brave in battle, he quickly rose up the ranks. He had discovered his passion, and he was getting wealthier in the process. His childhood dream was coming true.

Then Queen Anne's War ended in 1713. Unfortunately for Edward and thousands of privateers, they were now unemployed. Many continued to do what they did best and raided foreign ships. They were now labeled as "pirates." Edward, for one, did not care about a treaty between the neighboring countries. He was committed to plundering ships, and he would see it through to the end. If he was to be called a pirate, then a pirate he would be.

Edward traveled to the pirate island of New Providence in the Caribbean where he came in contact with the leader of a pirate fleet. His name was Benjamin Hornigold. Hornigold was the self-proclaimed "governor" of the pirate stronghold.

Captain Hornigold put Edward in charge of a small six-gun sloop and a crew of seventy pirates to sail alongside his flagship, the thirty-six-gun *Ranger*. Together they terrorized the Caribbean waters. One day they seized a rich French slave ship. In addition to his shares of the plunder, Hornigold rewarded Edward's courage by putting him in command of the big prize. Edward immediately freed the slaves, recruited the crew members, rearmed the decks with forty guns, and patriotically renamed her *Queen Anne's Revenge*.

Edward Teach was beginning to carve his name and reputation across the Atlantic Ocean as the infamous "Blackbeard."

• • •

BLACKBEARD STOOD ON the stern of *Queen Anne's Revenge* watching his crew prepare for battle as the British Royal Navy warship *Scarborough* sailed closer.

He said to his first mate, "Israel, fetch my weapons."

"Here's your lucky coat, Captain," said Israel Hands, helping Blackbeard put on his long scarlet brocaded coat and fastened it tightly with a wide black belt around his waist. The large silver belt buckle was shaped in the form of a skull. Then he inserted his trusty cutlass and dagger into his belt. Israel was too short to help slip two holster-like leather straps over Blackbeard's head that crisscrossed his big bear chest—each fitted to hold three pistols. Blackbeard adjusted the holsters and said, "My pistols."

"Aye, aye, Captain," said Israel, handing Blackbeard each of his six silver-inlaid pistols that were half-cocked and ready for firing.

Once all of his weaponry was in place, Blackbeard stuck his well-worn tri-corne hat over his dirty black hair that he wore braided in a dozen long pigtails. Along with his long black beard that was plaited into tails tied off with colorful ribbons, he looked like a hairy creature from the deep blue sea.

And if the look of this giant walking arsenal was not enough to scare you, Blackbeard did the most unusual thing. He inserted long, slow-burning hemp cords that were normally used to ignite the powder in the ship's cannons under his hat; and he lit them! The cords burned very slowly, and the smoke encircled his head.

"Light me up!" ordered Blackbeard.

"Captain, this is crazy," said Israel, putting a match to the end of the long cords.

"I learned as a boy that sailors are very superstitious," said Blackbeard, laughing as the smoke was swirling around his bearded face. "And when they see what looks like the devil coming at them, they will surrender their booty without a shot fired."

"Shot fired," shouted Black Caesar, as the sound of cannon fire screamed across the water. Seconds later, the shot splashed far forward off the bow of the *Queen Anne Revenge*.

The *Scarborough* fired a warning shot in hopes that the pirate warship would lower her black Jolly Roger flag (skull and crossbones) and surrender.

"Strike down the Jolly Roger," ordered Blackbeard with a shrewd smile. "But lower our black colors very slowly. I want those British tars to think we are surrendering as we close upon them port side."

"We are in range," said Philip Morton, the ship's master gunner, when the navy vessel was within accurate range of Blackbeard's big guns. "Gunners, hold steady and wait for my signal."

"Hoist the black flag," said Blackbeard. "And fire at will, gunner."

The gun crew expertly executed a broadside of cannon fire to roll down the side of the *Queen Anne's Revenge*. The rhythm and precision of the explosive guns shocked the naval warship into cover.

For hours the two warships exchanged cannon fire causing considerable dam-

age to both vessels. Lumber splintered in all directions, sails were shredded, masts and rigging toppled onto decks, and cannons exploded on impact. There were numerous deaths and crippling injuries on both sides. And eventually, the *Scarborough* ran out of ammunition and had to abandon her mission to rid the seas of Blackbeard and his pirate crew.

The weary crew of *Queen Anne's Revenge* raised their weapons and gave a collective cheer as they watched their dreaded enemy limp away to the horizon. They had outlived the hangman's noose another day and would steer to the American coastline to fill their bellies and pockets with rum and riches.

• • •

BLACKBEARD'S LEGEND SPREAD throughout the American colonies, and he took advantage of his notoriety.

"A sail. A sail!" shouted the lookout in the crow's nest.

"It looks to be a ten-gunner," said Black Caesar, lowering the spyglass, "and she is hoisting the black flag."

"I wonder what scoundrel be in these waters besides us?" asked Israel, standing at Blackbeard's side.

Instead of the normal single warning shot across the bow, *Queen Anne's Revenge* fired off a volley of three cannons to ensure the unnamed pirate vessel that her captain was welcome aboard. The gesture was also Blackbeard's subtle way of sending a message that *Queen Anne's Revenge* was a fully armed warship capable of massive destruction if need be.

"Toss the grappling irons," ordered Black Caesar as the smaller vessel came alongside Blackbeard's ship. "Boarding party, prepare to board. Muskets at the ready."

The crew hauled on the grappling lines securing the two ships together. Blackbeard's men lined the gunwales and climbed up in the rigging with muskets and pistols ready in case the visiting vessel did not follow their captain's commands.

"Ahoy," said Blackbeard, "From whence came you?"

"From the seas," replied a voice from the vessel, repeating the secret pirate code. Then the pirate identified the ship, "We sail the *Revenge*, captained by Major Stede Bonnet."

"Send him aboard," said Blackbeard. And then he turned his attention to Black Caesar. "Toss down a ladder and escort our brethren to my quarters."

"Shall I send a party aboard the *Revenge* to relieve her of any necessities?" asked Black Caesar, rubbing his hands together in anticipation of finding some tasty rum and beer.

"No," said Blackbeard, stroking his long black beard, "I have a better idea."

• • •

BLACKBEARD HAD NEVER met Major Stede Bonnet, the "Gentleman Pirate," but he had heard of him and his most bizarre pirating career.

"Welcome aboard, Major," said Blackbeard, gazing over the man's outfit. "I see you fit the gentlemanly reputation that has come before you."

"Why, thank you, Sir," replied Bonnet, who was clean-shaven and dressed as an English gentleman in a silver satin vest, white lace at his wrists, black breeches, and a white powdered wig atop of his head.

"Is it true," asked Blackbeard, "that you purchased your ship and paid your crew out of your own funds?"

"Yes, that I did, Sir," replied Bonnet, proudly.

Blackbeard then asked, "Why did you, a retired British Army Major, leave your lovely island plantation on Barbados to go on account as a pirate?"

"I tired of the idle life of a planter," replied Bonnet. "I sought adventure and excitement. But I am finding this life hard and the prizes to plunder not an easy task to complete."

Blackbeard walked around the captain's table and gently placed his arm around Bonnet's sloped shoulders and said kindly, "Major, you should make your quarters here in the comfort of the *Queen Anne's Revenge* as my guest. A refined gentleman, like yourself, is accustomed to better accommodations than the small trappings on the *Revenge*."

"Really?" asked Bonnet, surprised by Blackbeard's offer. "That is most gracious of you, Sir. But then who would sail my ship and lead my crew?"

"I will have one of my men captain your ship," said Blackbeard, "and we will sail both vessels together to plunder the Atlantic. I will also make sure that you receive your full captain's share of all spoils."

Major Bonnet quickly grabbed Blackbeard's hand and began shaking it vigorously. He said excitingly, "You have a deal!"

Blackbeard called the meeting to a close and held back Black Caesar and Israel until his guests left the cabin and were out of earshot.

"Captain," asked Black Caesar, puzzled, "why give this landlubber your quarters and a double share of the crew's plunder?"

"No worries," replied Blackbeard, "we now have his ship and crew to add to our fleet, and he has nothing but the sweat of my handshake. Now be gone and let us set sail to strike fear in the hearts of America."

• • •

ONE EARLY MORNING at the end of May, in the year 1718, Blackbeard sailed into the harbor of Charleston with a fleet of four pirate ships and more than four hundred dangerous men. It was the largest pirate navy ever assembled on the America coastline.

The beautiful blue harbor was bustling with merchant ships sailing to and from the capital city of South Carolina with their holds filled with cargo. Charleston was a major trading port in the Americas, so the addition of several more ships entering the protected waters would easily go unnoticed—especially since they were disguised as ordinary trading vessels. Blackbeard's ships flew England's Union Jack flag, the gunports were closed, the swivel guns in the bow and stern were secured tightly against the gunwales, and most of the crew was hidden below deck.

Blackbeard turned his attention away from the oncoming city and addressed the gathering of his fleet's captains, quartermasters, and navigators. "This here town has no idea what suffering is sailing into her waters."

"What are your plans, Captain?" asked Captain Richards.

Blackbeard had assigned Richard Richards to captain Bonnet's *Revenge* while the Major remained onboard *Queen Anne's Revenge* as his guest—more like an unaware prisoner.

"First and foremost," replied Blackbeard, "I intend to avoid the city's fort that lies south by heaving to the deeper channel north of the harbor's entrance. And second, we shall situate our ships strategically along the entrance to capture every vessel sailing into our blockade."

"What if one of them tries to outrun us, Sir?" asked Major Bonnet innocently.

"Put a blast of hot metal in her!" yelled Blackbeard. "But every one of my captains knows to dispatch a boarding party to plunder any valuables, biscuit, livestock, and spirits before she sinks."

"What about the crew and passengers?" asked the astonished Major Bonnet.

"You are right, Major," replied Blackbeard. "Transfer all passengers to your vessel, and we will ransom them for gold and silver. The crew, offer them work or clap them in irons if they refuse. And the captain, tie him to the mainmast and let him go down to Davy Jones's Locker with the ship."

On the third day of the historic blockade, Israel signaled the ships to open their gunports and hoist the black flags. The city of Charleston was now held hostage by pirates and its fate unknown.

One of the ships, a large merchantman named *Crowley*, had more than just coin and cargo removed from her possession. Captain Richards and five of his crew physically escorted a wealthy-looking gentleman and his son onto the deck of *Queen Anne's Revenge*.

"How dare you treat me in such a rough manner," said the gentleman angrily, as he was shoved forward onto the ship's deck. "I will see that you are all hanged!"

"Well, well, who do we have here?" asked Blackbeard, who had approached the party from the rear. "Who wants to see me dance at the end of an Admiralty rope?"

The gentleman turned to see Blackbeard hovering over him. He almost fainted. The young boy said bravely, "You let us be. We are on our way to England."

"Ha-ha," laughed Blackbeard. "No, boy, you are on your way to a nightmare."

"Captain, we discovered from the *Crowley* passenger list that there were some very important citizens onboard," said Captain Richards. "And I would like to present to you the honorable Samuel Wragg of the Carolina Governor's Council and his son, William."

"Mr. Wragg," said Blackbeard, "we shall see how important you really are. And, son, you should join my crew if you are as brave as your tongue. Take them to my cabin now."

Israel Hands had a map laid out across the chart table showing Captain Richards and Captain John Archer the waters around their hideout in Pamlico Sound. Black Caesar was showing Captain Charlie Sorg a new cutlass that he had removed from one of the prizes. And Blackbeard was mixing a helping of gunpowder from his pouch into a mug of rum, which he lit and poured down his gullet. Major Bonnet stared in open-mouth amazement.

"Your turn, Major," said Blackbeard, holding up a pewter mug for Bonnet. "Join me in a drink of kill-devil."

Blackbeard laughed, wiped his shaggy whiskers with the back of his hand, and said, "Now that we have the harbor blocked off, several ships confiscated, our

hold full of booty, and these important citizens aboard, we must decide the terms from the city of Charleston. What do we demand as ransom from this fair city?"

"I do not know about ransom, Captain," said Black Caesar, stabbing his sword into the wooden deck. "But I do know the Yellow Jack bug bit them but good."

"Captain, there is some strange pox on this ship as well," said Israel Hands. "The ship's surgeon tells me there is no medicine and ointments."

"Israel, be off and tell the surgeon to create a list of the medicines we need," ordered Blackbeard.

Blackbeard returned his attention to the prisoners before him.

"Mr. Wragg, I plan to send two of my men ashore with a demand that your Carolina governor supply us with medicines," said Blackbeard. "And you will accompany them to ensure my message is delivered. Because if I do not get my medicines and my crew does not return, I shall order all prisoners put to death and their heads sent to Governor Johnson—including his." Blackbeard pointed to young William.

The boy massaged his neck with his right hand while staring gallantly at the strange creature before him.

"What if the city will not allow Wragg to return?" asked Captain John Archer of the *Adventure*. "Him sitting on the city council. Maybe we should send another prisoner?"

"Capital idea, Archer," said Blackbeard, pacing around the cabin. "Mr. Wragg, who do you suggest we send that will convey the grave danger that you and your son and your fellow citizens are presently in?"

"I think Master Marks," replied Mr. Samuel Wragg grudgingly. "He is well respected throughout the Carolinas."

"Richards, you make ready with your first mate and longboat crew to row Master Marks ashore," continued Blackbeard, as he removed his long scarlet coat from a hook on the wall. "Richards, wrap my coat around Master Marks so the Carolina folks know who is making this ransom demand. And you let them know their town will be flooded in this bloody color if my conditions are refused."

• • •

SAMUEL WRAGG SAT on the small bunk with his chin resting in the palms of his hands with a worried look across his brow, while young William was franticly searching through the first mate's cabin.

"What are you looking for, William?" asked Mr. Wragg.

"There has to be something in here that we can use to unlock the door," replied William.

"Are you insane, boy!" said Mr. Wragg. "We are in enough of a pickle!"

"Father," replied William, "if we do not escape I think that pirate Blackbeard will follow through with his promises and cut our heads off." Then holding up a

pair of charting navigational dividers, he said excitedly, "Look what I found! This should do the trick. If we get this door open, we can swim to the sandbar at the harbor's entrance."

William knelt down on one knee and carefully stuck one of the two pointed ends of the instrument into the keyhole. He poked and prodded and twisted the dividers in the locking mechanism for a couple of minutes with sweat dripping from his forehead. Suddenly, an audible click was heard.

"Father, I did it!" exclaimed William, pulling the device out of the keyhole.

"Good work, son," said Mr. Wragg, patting William on the back. "Let me peek out to make sure no one is around."

"I want to look too," said William, putting the dividers in his pocket.

Very, very slowly, Mr. Wragg opened the cabin door without making a sound. Once a sliver of daylight appeared between the door and the doorframe, he peaked through the crack. William, who remained crouched down, glanced out through the opening from his angle. They saw nothing except the empty hall-way in front of the first mate's cabin. Mr. Wragg very carefully opened the door far enough to stick his head out. And so did William.

"What are you two doing!?" yelled the ship's cook, who just at that very moment was turning the corner carrying a pewter pot of salmagundi from the galley.

"Ahhhh!" screamed Mr. Wragg, startled, and hit his head on the door edge in surprise.

"We needed some air," replied William cleverly.

The peg-legged cook chuckled, "Wise kid. Now if Blackbeard finds this here door open, he will stuff the two of you lubbers in barrels and fill them with rats. Sir, have you ever seen what hungry rats do to men, and *boys*, when they are confined inside a barrel?"

Mr. Wragg and William backed into the cabin and sat on the bunk as the cook walked directly over to the first mate's sea locker and retrieved two fancy ceramic bowls.

"Here," said the cook, dishing out two bowls of turtle-based stew. "I hope for your sake my slop is not your last meal."

Samuel Wragg and William suffered the following two days confined to the closet-size cabin. The thought of rats nibbling on their eyes and ears was enough to prevent any further attempts at escape.

William woke up on the floor of the first mate's cabin to the sounds of yelling and movement outside the door. He crawled over to the door and peered out through the keyhole in hopes of discovering what all the fuss was about.

Up on the quarterdeck, Black Caesar watched through a spyglass Captain Richards returning in the ship's longboat with his first mate and Master Marks, who was still wearing the oversized scarlet coat. He had a wooden chest resting on his lap.

Master Marks was escorted to Blackbeard's cabin, where the chest was opened and the ship's surgeon verified the chest's medical contents. Blackbeard instructed Israel Hands to signal the other pirate ships to release the nine captured ships and all of the crew and passengers. The ships were plundered clean of all cargo. And the gentlemen prisoners had to return to the city of Charleston half-naked because the pirates were now strutting around the fleet's decks wearing their fine clothing and jewelry.

Israel unlocked the door to his quarters and addressed the two prisoners with his right hand behind his back. "You are free to go," he said. "Our demands have been met. But heed my warning, if there is one item missing from my quarters, we will be back in the dead of night in *your* bedrooms to claim it. And the 'we' is me and these." Israel brought his hand forward showing a cage holding two huge rats. "The cook found me two nasty ones in the galley that he thought might like to visit you."

• • •

FEAR SPREAD ALONG the entire American seaboard following news of Blackbeard's bold blockade of Charleston. Governors from every coastal city from Boston to South Carolina began making military preparations to ward off or capture the bloodthirsty Blackbeard. Except the colony of North Carolina.

Blackbeard was known among the North Carolina townsfolk. He sailed their waterways and sold much of his plundered cargo in its coastal towns over the past year. The merchants enjoyed his discounted hard-to-get merchandise. And the governor of the colony, Charles Eden, turned a blind eye toward his citizens doing business with the cutthroat pirates. In fact, he granted Blackbeard a "Royal Pardon"—which ensured that he would escape the hangman's noose, as long as he retired from his pirating ways—and offered a gift of several barrels of sugar and cocoa.

Blackbeard had no intention of living on the right side of the law. Once a pirate, always a pirate. He blatantly lied to the governor and maintained a respectable presence in the North Carolina town of Bath Town while he contin- ued to plunder shipping from a hideout off neighboring Ocracoke Island.

Unbeknownst to Blackbeard, the colony of Virginia to the north was making pirate hunting a priority. Governor Alexander Spotswood was so disgusted with Governor Eden's lack of action that he posted a reward and commissioned two Royal Navy warships, HMS *Pearl* and HMS *Lyme*, which were stationed at the

mouth of the James River, to protect his colony, to sail south and destroy the pirate nest before it turned into another pirate stronghold.

"Lieutenant Maynard," asked Governor Spotswood, "what is the progress of our secret pirate-hunting plan? When will you be ready to attack?"

"The *Pearl* and *Lyme* warships are presently providing the two sloops with crew, weapons, and ammunition," replied Maynard. "But we cannot take any of the ships' big guns for fear of being weighed down and hindering our ability to navigate the winding and shallow waters around Blackbeard's hideout. So we should be ready by the next high tide."

"As an added incentive to the crew," said Governor Spotswood, "I have placed a bounty on the heads of Blackbeard and his crew—dead or alive. Do not fail me, and you and your men will be well rewarded."

"Thank you, Sir," said Maynard. "We will bring you back the pirate's head!"

While Maynard was making preparations, Blackbeard was laying low in his eight-gun *Adventure* in the waters within Pamlico Sound. The blockade of South Carolina had made him public enemy number one, so he developed a mischievous strategy to disband most of his pirate fleet and then disappear.

First, Blackbeard sent Major Bonnet and the crew of the *Revenge* on a phony assignment to Bath Town to call on the governor for a Royal Pardon. Next, he mercilessly ran his warship *Queen Anne's Revenge* into a sandbar off North

Carolina and stranded all but fifty of his most ruthless rogues. These men then helped him transfer ammunition, supplies, and all of the plundered treasure onto the *Adventure* to the distress of the marooned crew. Finally, he sailed the *Adventure* to his undisclosed hideaway on the western side of Ocracoke Island.

Most of Blackbeard's crew was having a good time ashore in Bath Town with only a skeleton crew onboard the *Adventure*. The pirates were drinking, playing cards, and entertaining several sailors from a local trading sloop. They had become lazy and complacent during the months of inactivity, and they neglected to post a lookout out on the island to warn of any intruders on the morning of November 22, 1718.

"Weigh anchor," Lieutenant Maynard said to the crews of the two sloops, *Ranger* and *Jane*. "Follow the lead of our longboat. We do not want to be grounded in these unfamiliar waters."

A four-oared longboat took readings of the depths of the waterways, slowly winding their way around the tip of Ocracoke Island about a mile away from the anchored *Adventure*. At that point, one of Blackbeard's crew yelled "Ships ahoy!"

Blackbeard stumbled up from the ship's hold and grabbed a spyglass and said, "Gunner make ready for battle. They cannot be one of us. I see no teeth behind their ports."

"Man the guns!" screamed Philip Morton, the master gunner. "Quick with

the swivel gun! Let's put a scare into these intruders."

The tired pirates snapped out of their sleepiness and hurried across the deck to the sloop's four big guns on both broadsides to prep them with powder, wadding, and iron round-shot. One of the crew hustled to the smaller swivel gun mounted on the bow of the sloop with a bag of scrap metal and small round-shot.

Blackbeard pointed to the swivel gun and nodded.

Gunner Morton yelled, "Fire!"

The swivel gun shot a warning spray of smoke and projectiles toward the longboat. A scream from the local pilot manning the boat could be heard echoing across the morning mist. The oarsmen suddenly halted their forward direction and quickly rowed behind the cover of the two sloops that slowly weaved their way toward the *Adventure*.

The two sloops without cannons had to maneuver close enough to the *Adventure* to engage their enemy with small-arms fire. At this point the mission appeared suicidal, so to motivate his men, Lieutenant Maynard ordered, "Hoist our King's colors!" He called as the Union Jack Flag was raised on both ships. "Keep your heads low. We may have to man the oars to get close enough in these shallow waters."

"Hoist the black flag," said Blackbeard to Black Caesar preparing for battle. "I want these royal tars to see that death awaits them. Cut the anchor and slowly drift to port through that narrow channel to show them our starboard teeth," said Blackbeard. "They do not know these waters, and we will lay them upon a hidden sandbar. And then we will blow them to bits."

The *Jane* and *Ranger* tacked their way through the watery switchbacks closer to Blackbeard's position, falling into his trap. The *Ranger* ran aground. They were within hailing distance of the *Adventure*. Blackbeard yelled across the calm water, "Who are you villains? I will neither give nor take quarter."

"You see from our colors that we are not pirates," replied Maynard. "And I expect no quarter, nor will I give you quarter."

Blackbeard's fierce temper rose. He ordered, "Gunner Morton, give them a taste of our metal."

"Starboard guns, fire!" said Gunner Morton.

The *Ranger,* which was wedged in the mud, was the closer of the two naval sloops, and its deck was blasted with a broadside of scrap metal and musket balls killing everyone in its wake. Blackbeard then focused his attention on the empty decks of the *Jane*. The odds had shifted heavily in his favor.

At the sound of the *Adventure*'s cannons discharge, Maynard and his crew hit the deck. They felt the impact of the blast and its devastating effects as debris from the *Ranger* scattered across their deck. When he peeked above the gunwales, Maynard saw bodies strewn all over the destroyed *Ranger* with no one at the helm.

"Stay on course," Maynard ordered the terrified pilot. "We must come alongside Blackbeard's ship before he reloads his guns." He then ordered most of his crew to scurry down belowdecks so that it would appear to Blackbeard that the broadside had a devastating blow on his ship.

Even with less than his normal seasoned crew onboard, Blackbeard felt confident that victory was within his grasps. He believed he had one naval sloop disabled and a second undermanned, so now it was time to take the offensive.

"Turn toward the enemy," said Blackbeard. "It is time to take the fight to them. And offer no quarter! I want every sailor on that sloop dead!"

"Toss the grenadoes!" Blackbeard ordered, just seconds before the *Adventure* rammed into the *Jane*.

Several crew members lit the fuses and tossed hollow cast-iron balls filled with gunpowder and tiny pieces of metal onto the deck of the *Jane*. They exploded on impact resulting in a blinding display of smoke and sending splinters of metal in all directions.

The *Adventure* collided alongside the *Jane* and immediately grappling irons were thrown and hooked to her gunwales. The lines were made tight to secure the two ships together.

"Follow me, men! Let's jump onboard and cut them to pieces!" screamed Blackbeard, leading the charge as he and his crew swung onboard the *Jane* with cutlasses and boarding axes raised to finish off any sailors still alive.

But as soon as the pirates hit the smoke-filled, slippery deck, they heard a voice echo from the sloop's hold, "Charge!"

The Royal Navy crew came pouring up from belowdecks yelling, firing pistols, and hacking with swords at the ambushed pirates. Lieutenant Maynard made his way through the battle toward his archrival, who was slashing and stabbing every sailor in sight. "Blackbeard," said Maynard, stabbing at him with his sword, "your time of terror has ended."

"Ha-ha," laughed Blackbeard in a booming voice, countering Maynard's thrust with a powerful downward stroke of his large cutlass and cutting Maynard's sword in half. "You are no match for me, and I will see you bleed to death."

Maynard quickly backed up, threw the broken sword at Blackbeard, drew his pistol, and fired. The shot wounded Blackbeard, but it did not stop him.

"You are mine!" said Blackbeard, continuing to advance toward Maynard with his cutlass raised over his head. And just at the moment when he was within striking range, a sailor stabbed him in the back of the neck. Blackbeard turned to defend against the unknown attacker with blood squirting everywhere. "Take this," said Maynard, who had picked up a stray sword and stabbed Blackbeard in the side during the distraction.

"Ahhh," screamed Blackbeard, recovering and attacking Maynard with a giant

slash of his cutlass. Luckily for Maynard, the blood loss had weakened Blackbeard's blow, and it just missed his head. Before Blackbeard could recover from his attacking strike, he was stabbed by another sailor. Then shot by another. But still he fought on until Maynard's crew surrounded the monster and shot him a total of five times and stabbed him twenty times before he fell to the deck.

Seeing their captain down, the remaining battle-weary pirates cried out, "Quarter! Quarter!"

"Good quarter granted," ordered Maynard, picking up a sword. "No more killing. Put them in irons. They will have time to think of death before they meet the hangman's noose."

Then Maynard lifted his sword and with one vicious two-handed stroke, he cut off Blackbeard's big head. "Throw the body overboard. And hang the devil's head from the ship's bowsprit as a warning to all pirates. We will show the world that Blackbeard is dead."

The End